Bud's Nap

by Bobby Lynn Maslen
pictures by John R. Maslen

Scholastic Inc.
New York   Toronto   London   Auckland   Sydney

Also available:

Bob Books
for Beginning Readers

More Bob Books
For Young Readers

For more Bob Books ask for them at your local bookstore or call: 1-800-733-5572.

ISBN 0-590-22443-3

12 11 10 9 8 7 6 5 4 3 2   4 5 6 7 8 9/9

Printed in the U.S.A.   10

First Scholastic printing, October 1994

Bud sat under a big green tree. Bud was sleepy. Bud had a nap.

Three bees buzzed and the queen bee buzzed. The bees saw Bud sitting under the tree.

Bud snoozed. Bud was fast asleep.

The bees buzzed around Bud.
Bud snoozed. Bud snored.

Bud did not see the bees.
The bees did see Bud.

The bees flew close. Bud snoozed
on. Bud snored more.

A bee sat on Bud's knee.
A bee sat on Bud's hat.
A bee sat on Bud's hand.

Bud did
   not feel the bees. He did not move.
Bud snoozed and snored even more.

The bees flew off. The bees flew
from buttercup to buttercup.

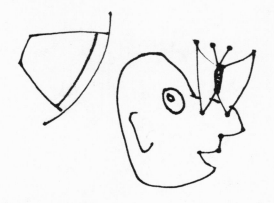

A butterfly flew by. The butterfly saw Bud. The butterfly sat
on Bud's nose. Suddenly Bud woke up!

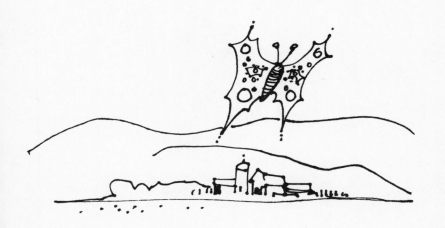

The bees buzzed on in the butter-
cups. The butterfly flew into the sky.

Bud did not see the bees. He did not
see the butterfly. Bud jumped up.
He did not feel sleepy anymore.

The End

Book 3 adds:

Long Vowel Combination:
ee   -   green

Vowel Combination:
oo   -   snoozed

Blend:
qu   -   queen